Clara Vulliamy

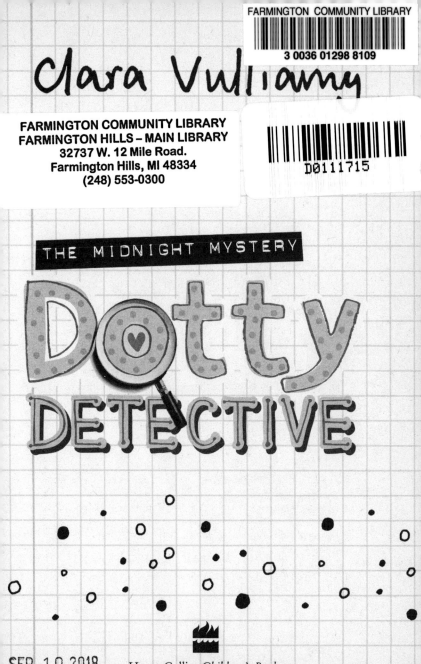

THE MIDNIGHT MYSTERY

Dotty DETECTIVE

HarperCollins *Children's Books*

First published in Great Britain by
HarperCollins *Children's Books* in 2017
First published in the United States of America in this edition by
HarperCollins *Children's Books* 2018
HarperCollins *Children's Books* is a division of
HarperCollins*Publishers* Ltd,
HarperCollins Publishers
1 London Bridge Street
London SE1 9GF

The HarperCollins website address is:
www.harpercollins.co.uk

18 19 20 21 LSC 10 9 8 7 6 5 4 3 2 1

ISBN 978-0-00-826916-6

Typeset in Archer 16/24pt
Printed and bound in the United States of America by
LSC Communications

Find out more about HarperCollins and the environment at
www.harpercollins.co.uk/green

for my ACE MUM! with lots of love

Read the whole series:

**This book
belongs to...**

DOT

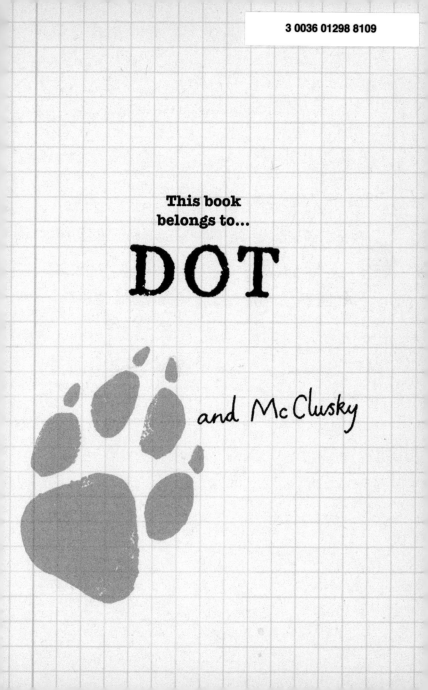

and McClusky

Sunday

This is me!

My real name is Dorothy Constance Mae Louise, but that's a bit of a mouthful so I just like to be called Dot.

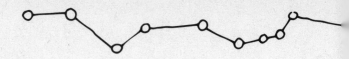

I might SEEM as if I have an ordinary sort of life. I live with my mom, the twins (my brother and sister, Alf and Maisy), and my dog, McClusky...

and I go to Oakfield School.

BUT **THAT'S** NOT ALL... Me and McClusky and my best pal, Beans, have our very own super-secret, super-sleuthing detective agency: the JOIN THE DOTS DETECTIVES!

However murky the mystery or fiendishly puzzling the problem, we can **ALWAYS** piece together the clues and solve the case. It's like a really complicated join the dots puzzle: only at the *end* can you see the whole picture.

Here is my bedroom—check out the amazing chandelier Mom gave me!

This isn't just my bedroom, though, **OH NO**. It's also the Join the Dots Detectives HQ, where I do all my best deductivizing, head scratching, and end-of-pencil chewing when I am on a case and studying the clues.

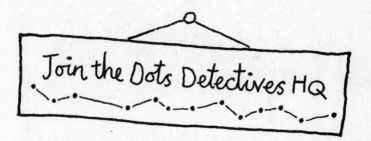

I keep all my treasures here too. LOTS of boxes, packed full to bursting with all my special things.

Mom says it drives her CRAZY that we all have *TOO MUCH STUFF* in our family.

Although one look at her collection of unusual teapots

and it is clear that she has A LOT of stuff too.

The twins have their own weird collections...

and, when me and Mom move the furniture to do the vacuuming, we discover that McClusky has been hoarding HIS "treasures" too, behind the sofa.

"So that's where my knitting yarn has gone to!" says Mom.

McClusky's embarrassed face!

Monday

Coconut Crunchies for breakfast!

YESSSSSS!!!

It's my **BEST** and **FAVORITE** cereal. I do the maze on the back of the box.

Mom says, "A new week!" and turns over a page on our wall calendar. It says, *Life is a gift—enjoy every moment!*

But the twins are enjoying every moment of putting on all their clothes **COMPLETELY INSIDE OUT** a bit too much, so now we are in a HUGE rush to get to school on time.

Lining up in the playground to go into our classrooms, there is only one thing everybody is talking about...

On Wednesday we are going on a school trip! **THREE WHOLE DAYS** at ADVENTURE CAMP!!!

"I haven't been away to any kind of camp before," says Amy nervously. "I wonder what it will be like?"

"I've been on **LOADS** of camps," Laura says, "and I've gone night-kayaking in the Amazon **AND** slept under the stars in the Arctic!"

Laura ALWAYS gets on our nerves.

I ignore Laura and say to Amy, "Me neither, but I am sure it's going to be *awesome!*"

"It's not as far as the Amazon,
but it's definitely a long way away,"
says Beans. *"TWO HOURS*
in the school bus!"

After attendance our teacher
Mr. Dickens is telling us more about
the trip.

Mr. D tells us that we will be put into
groups for sleeping, with separate
cabins for girls and for boys.

PLEASE,
PLEASE,
PLEASE *no snorers in*

my cabin, I am saying to myself!

ZZZZZZZZZZZ

We will also be put into different teams for the activities. There will be **points** given for each activity, and also for being helpful and tidy, and the team with the most points wins...

THE ACE ADVENTURERS' PRIZE!!!

ACE!

Laura says she has won first prize for snowboarding and for horse riding AND for rock climbing and she will **DEFINITELY** win the **ACE ADVENTURERS' PRIZE** too.

Mr. D is looking at the list of activities, making WOW faces and gasps of astonishment.

"The activities are **TOP SECRET** until we get there!" says Mr. D, creating a big show of turning the piece of paper face down on his desk so we cannot see. "But here's a little clue..."

Mr. D does his special suspense dance. He loves teasing us!

"We will have close encounters with **NATURE ON THE WILD SIDE**," he says, "and explore our spirit of **adventure!**"

This sounds amazing! Everybody is cheering.

Frankie Logan who sits at my table is overeager to show us his wild side and ends up falling off his chair.

"We will have

NIGHT-TIME ESCAPADES!"

Mr. D goes on.

Everybody is going crazy with excitement.

"And now," he says, holding up some jelly jars full of leaves—I can just make out something moving inside—"to get us in the mood for the **Adventure Camp Nature Trail...**

"Let's show some **love** for BUGS AND SLUGS!"

By now some people are **literally** screaming. What will it be like when we actually *get there???*

Breaktime and I'm heading out to the playground, but I forgot my tangerine so I go back to the classroom.

But when I walk in through the door...

I see Laura in the empty classroom. She has turned over the activities list on Mr. D's desk and she's **reading** it.

I get a **FUNNY FEELING**, beginning in my toes. Before she can see me, I quietly back out of the room and *rush* to find Beans.

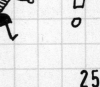

"Laura was sneaking a look at the list," I say to Beans. "It looked

VERY FISHY to me..."

"Sounds **SHADY** to me too," agrees Beans. "Why does she want to know what the activities are, ahead of everybody else?"

We don't know what to make of it. But one thing's for sure... when Laura is hatching one of her **DEVIOUS PLANS,** it always spells trouble for everybody else.

In the cafeteria, sitting with Amy and

Beans, Amy is still feeling **anxious** about the trip, so Beans cheers her up by sharing his pineapple chunks with her.

At the next table, Laura is writing in her sparkly pink secret notebook and looking over at us.

The funny feeling has reached my stomach. I don't like the look of this ONE BIT.

In Social Studies we are doing map-making. Beans is **genius** at maps. We make a key of *official* symbols:

FOOTPATH	- - - - - - - -	WALKS	
RAILWAY AND STATION		VIEWPOINT	
LIGHTHOUSE		CASTLE	
WOODS			
		POND	
GRASSLANDS			
CAMPSITE			

And we make up some of our own too...

LAURA   BEAR

EMERGENCY SNACKS

MYSTERY ???

MARSHMALLOWS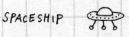

SPACESHIP

At going-home time Mr. D gives us all a reminder **PACKING LIST** to take home.

I still need to get a few **extremely important** things like toothpaste and a new raspberry-scented gel pen...so I ask Mom if we can walk home via the main street.

As we go past the pet-grooming parlor, Paws Awhile, I see a poster in the window:

This particularly catches my eye.
I look at the different categories...
Which could McClusky win?

He IS the most handsome dog in the
whole world, surely! Hmmmm, but he
does look as though he's been pulled
through a hedge backwards...I would
LOVE to buy him a new brush—and
there are bow ties for dogs too! SO
many to choose from! But I don't
have enough pocket money.

Maybe!

OH NO. I think McClusky would eat
it immediately!

But whatever his chances I will **DEFINITELY** enter McClusky into the Larks in the Park Dog Show. We will begin a *strict training program* tonight. Mom will have to take over while I'm away on **Adventure Camp**, though.

At home I decorate the packing list with my BEST stickers and put it up on the fridge with a polka-dot magnet.

ADVENTURE CAMP
PACKING LIST!
Don't forget:

raincoat   boots
sunscreen   indoor shoes
gloves   warm sweater
towel   pajamas
notebook   lots of socks
              toiletries

We have spaghetti for dinner. The twins are seeing who can make the most noise **slurping** up each strand.

"You have the table manners of a couple of piglets!" says Mom.

After supper I do Waggiest Tail practice with McClusky. For just *HALF* a Doggylicious biscuit let me tell you it's actually **IMPOSSIBLE** to count the wags!

I'm starting to pack my suitcase. Every time I check one thing off the packing list, I think of two new things to add.

AT LEAST 4 or 5 puzzle books

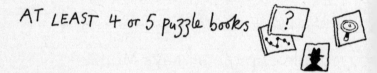

The BEST things from my stationery collection

VITAL to have barrettes in every color

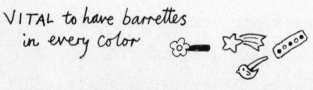

"Vital? REALLY?" says Mom, popping her head around the door.

Then she says, "Here—I've bought you a new toiletry bag for your trip!" It has cats wearing glasses on it, writing letters and numbers.

7
8
2
3   15
9
5
4
6   11
12
23

Mom says it's really a pencil case, but they are the same thing and no one will notice.

The twins wish they were going on **Adventure Camp**. They make a den out of sheets from the laundry basket...

and do

EXTREME

SPORTS

on the sofa,
even though they are not allowed
since they broke the springs
practicing the Olympic long jump.

At bedtime, I'm thinking about Laura acting strangely at school. Is she planning something SNEAKY???

boasting about
winning first prize

sneaking a look at the
top secret activities list

writing in her secret notebook

All **very** odd...

Trying new hairstyles helps me to relax. Doing my hair with one bobble...

and with three bobbles... but two is

BEST.

Tuesday

I need to talk to Beans again about Laura, but there is **NO TIME** because right after attendance it is PE in the playground.

We are practicing our

WILD-SIDE running.

We pretend we are running through the forest; dodging dangerous animals, deep rivers, and cliff edges.

Mr. D shouts out commands, like "JUMP OVER LOGS!" and

"DUCK UNDER BRANCHES!"

It is seriously full of perils. Joe falls into a "pit of snakes" and Beth is "carried off by a bear".

In quiet reading, we are finding it hard to concentrate. Just one day to go!!!

Beans whispers to me, "WHAT

CANDY ARE YOU BRINGING ON THE BUS? I AM BRINGING CHOCO CHOOS," and I whisper back, "SUPER-SOUR APPLE BALLS!"

We don't notice Mr. D is standing behind us. But instead of telling us off he whispers loudly, "AND I WILL

BE BRINGING TREACLE TOFFEE
BON-BONS."

In Health Mr. D talks to us about
being away from home. He tells us
that feeling worried or a bit homesick
is totally *fine* and nothing to be
embarrassed about.

Laura says she has been away from
home for **WEEKS AND WEEKS**
and doesn't get homesick *at all*.

Amy is very quiet.

I'm definitely going to miss Mom.

And I realize I haven't been away from McClusky for **three whole days**

EVER!

For dinner I ask Mom extra-nicely if we can have sausages so I can do some sausage-on-a-plate practice with McClusky.

He actually manages to catapult the sausage into the air, drop the plate, catch the sausage, and eat it; all in about ONE SECOND.

Impressive, but not *quite* what the judges are looking for.

After dinner I watch this week's episode of

FRED FANTASTIC— ACE DETECTIVE.

Me and Beans both think it is the best TV program **EVER**.

Fred is a detective who solves fiendishly tricky crimes by finding clues and piecing them together, just like the **JOIN THE DOTS DETECTIVES** do.

We *ALWAYS* follow **FRED FANTASTIC'S** five golden rules for solving a case:

1. **STAY FROSTY.**
This means STAY ALERT.
Fred Fantastic says this a lot.

2 FOLLOW THAT HUNCH!

Always listen to your instincts because they could lead to something.

3 USE YOUR NOODLE.

Use your brain—think!

4 LOOK FOR A LIGHT-BULB MOMENT.

A bright idea to help you suss things out.

5 GET PROOF.

You always need to have evidence before coming to any crafty conclusions.

In this episode a dastardly villain switches the road signs so that Fred and his cool sidekick, Flo, drive straight off the jetty and into the sea!

DOT'S ROOM

Now I MUST finish my packing!

I have to really

SQUEEEEEEEEEZE

everything into the suitcase and sit on it to get the lid shut.

polka-dot clothes

boots

polka-dot raincoat

cats-in-glasses toiletry bag

best pajamas with flamingos on

camera

sunglasses

stationery and puzzle books

"Would you like to borrow my wallaby woolly hat?" asks Mom.

"No more room!" I say. **PHEW* lucky escape!!!*

Cannot get to sleep. I am **EXCITED** *because I'm looking forward to Adventure Camp SO MUCH. But I am nervous too.*

Maybe it's nothing, but I still feel

UNEASY *about Laura.*

And I suddenly realize...

*Me and Beans need a really good way
to pass secret messages to each other
at* **Adventure Camp!** *Something
small, because we don't have space
in our suitcases to take our complete
detecting kit.*

*I look in my best code book for
inspiration, and I have the perfect
idea...*

A picture code!!

I make a special **picture code** *for us to use:*

a b c d e f g

h i j k l m n

o p q r s t u

v w x y z

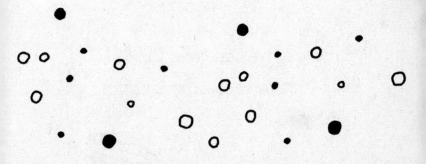

I write it twice: once for me and once for Beans. I just try it out to see if it works.

WEDNESDAY

We arrive at school very early in the morning. The bus is already waiting.

While the bags are being loaded on, I super-quickly show the picture code to Beans and give him his copy.

"This way we can send SECRET MESSAGES to each other, just in case..." I whisper.

"SUPER!" whispers Beans.

Mom gives me a **HUGE** hug,
then she and the twins and McClusky
are smiling and waving and tail-
wagging with the other families as
we all climb on board.

"Keep up the training practice,
McClusky!" I call out from the top step.

And we're OFF!

First there are **shrieks**, **whoops**, and **cheers**, then three different sing-alongs all at once, and we haven't even got around the corner yet!

Maybe too much candy has been eaten too quickly BECAUSE...

I don't even want to *think* about
what has just happened at the back,
but Mr. D jumps up and rushes down
the aisle with a paper bag. Me and
Amy sit together and play a good
game of **Fortunately–Unfortunately**.

"Fortunately our private jet lands on
a desert island," I say.

"Unfortunately we are immediately
surrounded by wolves!" says Amy.

"Fortunately the wolves
are very friendly and
bring us CAKE!" I say.

Amy is feeling a bit **shaky**. "Will there be wolves at **Adventure Camp?**" she asks.

"I'm SURE there won't be!" I reassure her.

AT LAST we arrive, and are greeted by super-friendly young grown-ups with **Ace Adventure Helper** written on their t-shirts.

With our outstandingly savvy new map skills we will soon find our way around!

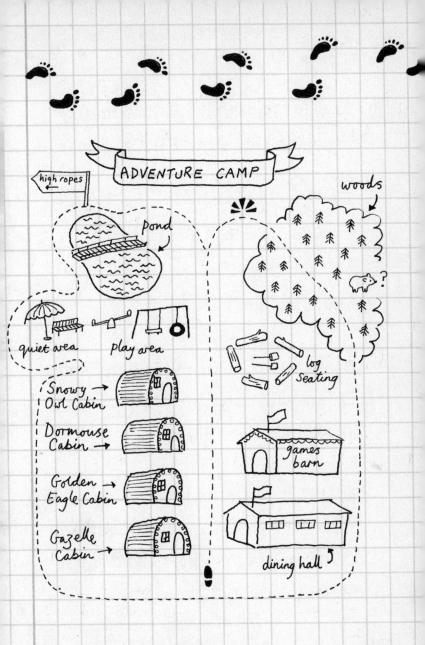

ADVENTURE CAMP

high ropes

pond

woods

quiet area

play area

log seating

Snowy Owl Cabin →

Dormouse Cabin →

Golden Eagle Cabin →

Gazelle Cabin →

games barn

dining hall

59

I am in Gazelle Cabin. I'm sharing my cabin with Amy, Kirstie, Alisha and (OH NO!!!!!)

Laura and her friend Ruby.

Beans is next door, in Golden Eagle Cabin, with Joe, Fiyaz, Marcus, Milo, and Frankie.

I **JUST** have time while no one is looking to write a quick **picture code** message to Beans and slip it under the door of his cabin...

There are three sets of bunk beds
and three small cupboards next to
each bunk. I am sharing bunks with
Alisha.

We have to make our own beds, which includes putting the duvet covers on— NO EASY TASK, I can tell you...

My duvet is **big** and **lumpy** up one end but empty at the other, and Alisha has completely disappeared inside hers, blundering around like a noisy snowman!

Unpacking, I find in the pocket of my favorite jeans a photo of me and McClusky!

Missing you already!
Mum xxx

Mom must have put it in my suitcase when I wasn't looking! I am **SO HAPPY**. I put it safely under my pillow.

Amy has brought a **cuddly** toy mouse called Mouse. Laura and Ruby are looking over at Mouse and I can see that behind their hands they are laughing.

We walk over to the dining hall for lunch, which is a buffet of all kinds of sandwiches, and yogurts for dessert.

Mr. D has changed into a

WILD

orange-and-yellow tracksuit. He looks like a **CRAZY** fruit salad.

He tells us our teams for the activities—I am with Alisha, Beans, and Joe.

There is a scoreboard written up with colored chalk. Everybody is asking, "Who will win the **ACE ADVENTURERS' PRIZE???**"

The afternoon activity is announced: a high ropes course!

"Points are given for *SPEED*, but also for being good team players and encouraging each other," our Ace Adventure Helpers tell us.

We get into our teams, put on our helmets and safety harnesses and away we go!

Up the Jacob's Ladder...

across the rope bridge...

wobble

wobble

and—

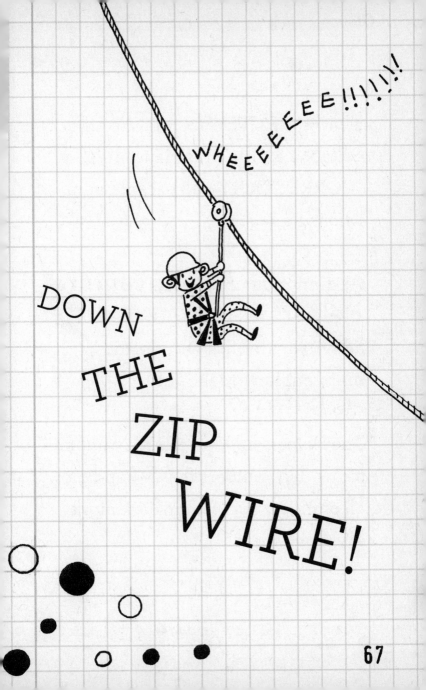

WHEEEEEEE!!!!!!

DOWN THE ZIP WIRE!

67

That was **EXTREMELY** fun! We all collapse on the grass laughing. *CORRECTION*—all except Laura, who is oddly quiet.

At dinner our Ace Adventure Helpers tell us about our evening activity: campfire stories and marshmallow-toasting!

The Helpers build a fantastic campfire for us. Tiny embers float up and glow all orange-y against the dark night sky.

We sit in a circle around the fire
toasting our marshmallows, and each
team chooses a person to tell a story.

First Beth tells a really good story about a beluga whale who plays the

bongos.

Then Fiyaz tells a **CRAZY** story about a hundred-metre-wide doughnut from space landing on top of Oakfield School.

Our team has chosen ME! I tell everyone that mine will be a **SPOOKY** story. And so I begin...

"There was once an old falling-down house with boarded-up windows and nobody lived there, but in the **dead of night** sometimes you can hear—"

Then all of a sudden Laura starts **coughing** loudly.

I continue: "You can hear a strange *wailing* noise and see—"

cough cough

"and see a glimmer of candlelight moving through the cracks—"

* cough cough cough*

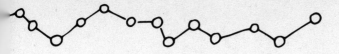

I try to continue with my story, but Laura starts complaining: "The campfire is **too smoky!**" I see her nudging Ruby, who starts coughing too.

"OH NO!" say the Helpers. "Perhaps we need to finish up here and call it a day."

So I never get to finish my story.

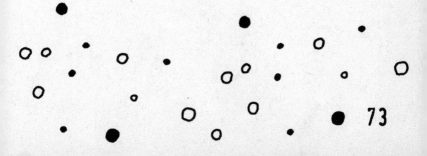

"That was really **bad luck**, Dot,"
says Mr. D. I do get some points for
trying, but on the scoreboard our
team are quite near the bottom now.
We are VERY disappointed.

 It must be the middle of the night.
I am woken by a noise...

I super-quietly get out of bed
and creep to the door. There's a
piece of paper on the floor—it's
a message from Beans!

Laura is **SO SNEAKY!!!!**

I must speak to Beans about this tomorrow at breakfast.

Thursday

Up and dressed and into the cafeteria for breakfast. I help myself to bread rolls and jam and pile up a plate with fruit. **Yummy!**

I sit with Beans for a super-hasty **JOIN THE DOTS DETECTIVES** meeting.

"Laura MUST have ruined my spooky campfire story on purpose!" I say. "But why?"

"What if she is trying to stop us winning points so that SHE can win the **ACE ADVENTURERS' PRIZE?**" says Beans.

"Yes, I am certain you're right! But before we can be sure, we need proof. This is a case for the Join the Dots Detectives!" I say. "We must **USE OUR PEEPERS** to see what she is planning next."

ON THE CASE

"**STAY FROSTY**, Dot!" says Beans.

"**STAY FROSTY**, Beans!" I say back.

Mr. D comes in with a **big** box. Everyone has a letter from home!

Mine is a card with two elephants riding a tandem bicycle on it, and it says...

Dear Dot,

We hope you are having an **AWESOME** time at Adventure Camp!

Don't worry about McClusky's training. I'm sure he will win the Dog Show. AND he will have a surprise to show you when you get home.

See you on Friday—can't wait!

With lots and lots of LOVE,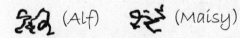

Mom,

     (Alf)   (Maisy)

and   (McClusky)

XXXX

A SURPRISE?

How mysterious!

But no time to think about that now...

We are going grass

tobogganing!!!

SUCH a **big** climb up the hill—it's practically Mount Everest. SO WINDY at the top, but totally worth it...

I have two turns on my own and one sharing a toboggan with Alisha—we are as squished together as sardines!

Amy is a **bundle of nerves,** but luckily she is in Kirstie's team so they go in a toboggan together too.

HURTLING down the hill *bump
bump bump*—very fast and
VERY FUN!

OOPS! Going too fast!

Lunch is pizza and salad.

DELISH!

Mr. D is having a BUSY DAY sorting things out...

Fiyaz's tooth has fallen out and he can't find it, Lily is walking with a mysterious limp, and the wind has blown Marcus's hat away.

We can just see it in a nearby field, being trampled on by a cow.

Our afternoon activity is the **Adventure Camp Nature Trail**, around the pond and into the Sensory Garden.

Joe steps nearly up to his knees in a **mucky puddle**.

At least Amy's happy that there's no sign of wolves, but we DO see some frogspawn, a pebble with a hole in it, and an earwig.

Beans calls the earwig Norman
and wonders if he can take it home.
But Norman crawls off and I have a
feeling we will never see him again.

Now we reach the

Sensory Path.

We have bare feet and a blindfold,
so we can experience everything
using our senses of touch and smell.

I explore the feeling of bark chips
under my feet, the smell
of mud and grass, and

*sniff

sniff*

something else...

It is Joe's

OLD SOGGY SOCKS,

taken off and abandoned. A pretty

powerful

sensory

experience

in itself.

After dinner our evening activity is announced:

a moonlight walk!

"When it is completely dark," the Ace Adventure Helpers tell us, "each team will be given a flashlight. Then we will go out into the night and listen out for **OWLS AND BATS!**"

"But please take extra care when moving around," they say. "It gets REALLY **dark** out there at night!"

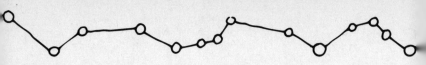

Each team has a special pack, laid out on the table, which includes:

a notebook

a pencil

a flashlight

But when I've cleared away my plate and cup and go to get our team pack...

our flashlight has

COMPLETELY

DISAPPEARED!

I see LAURA is lurking nearby.

Other teams' flashlights are

MISSING too.

I make a

**THIS
IS
URGENT**

face at Beans
and he makes a

YES IT IS face back,

but there's no time to talk because we
are all desperately searching for the
missing flashlights.

But no luck—no sign of them **anywhere**.

The Helpers say we cannot do the moonlight walk if some teams don't have flashlights.

SO

disappointing.

We all moan and groan, Laura loudest of all.

We all troop into the Games Barn instead.

The Helpers bring trays of yummy **hot chocolate** for us, and their guitars for a

sing-along.

...mmmmm......

Who knew Mr. D was **such** a **GENIUS** on the tambourine?!

At bedtime we are just heading back to our cabins. They look really pretty with string lights around the door.

At least the mystery limp is solved...

It turns out Lily and Amber have the same shoes but in **different** sizes, so they thought it would be fun to each wear one big one and one little one.

"You're a **STRANGE** group," says Mr. D, shaking his head and laughing.

We are all getting ready for bed.

Laura and Ruby are whispering in their bunk and rustling bags of chips. It sounds as though they're having a midnight feast. I wonder where they got their snacks from?

Amy is feeling a bit **shaky** again. "Are there any bears in these woods?" she asks.

I hear Laura and Ruby stifling **sniggers**.

Me, Kirstie, and Alisha all sit on Amy's bunk and chat about other things to distract her. None of us remembered to bring a **midnight**

feast, but Kirstie shares half a bag of pink chocolate penguins left over from the bus trip.

Mr. D pops his head around the door to tell us it's time for lights out. He also tells us that the flashlights DID turn up in the end—in a box, hidden under hundreds of BAGS OF CHIPS!!!

When I'm sure everyone is asleep,
I write a note to Beans using the
picture code.

I pop my head out of our cabin, check
the COAST IS CLEAR and slip the
note under his door.

I am sure that Laura will stop at *nothing* to **WIN** the **ACE ADVENTURERS' PRIZE!**

And as Fred Fantastic always says, **FOLLOW THAT HUNCH!**

 We have TWO clues: first the campfire story sabotage, now the hidden flashlights. But we can only solve this case when we have **PROOF**.

I'm doing a word search in my puzzle book under the covers, but I can hardly concentrate.

Tomorrow is our last day. Our last chance to win some points.

Our last chance to solve the CASE OF THE ACE ADVENTURERS' PRIZE!

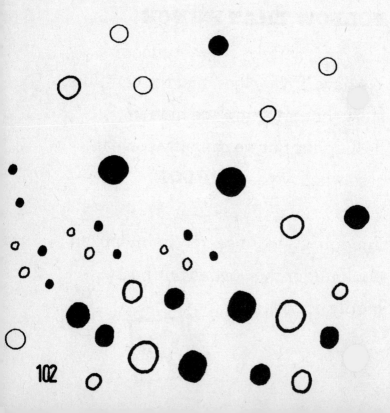

FRIDAY

Up early, and the sun is shining.

The final activity is announced...

THE EXTREME SPORTS CHALLENGE!!

There are **big** points to be won.

The whistle goes and with a mighty **cheer** the challenge begins.

The first challenge is

GLADIATORS
WITH
INFLATABLES.

We are each paired against someone from another team. We get up on to a bounce house platform and have to knock our opponent off it using a

GIANT
inflatable fruit!

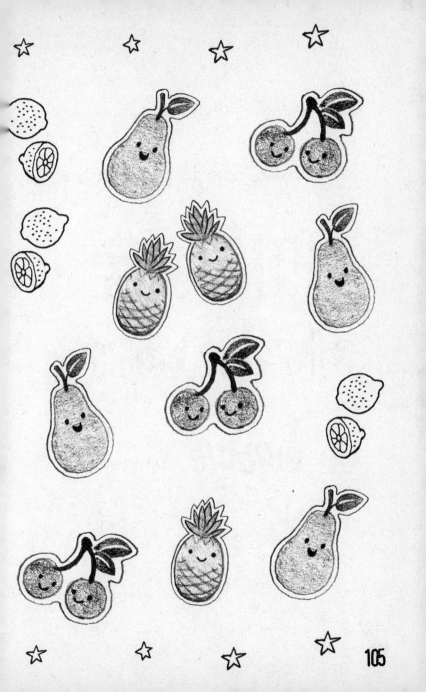

I am paired against Nadia.

She NEARLY knocks me off with a

HUGE

strawberry

and I **WObble** on the edge...

But then I JUST get in a good move
with my **giant cucumber**
and Nadia falls off. She is **laughing**.
Nadia is a good sport.

The second challenge is wiggling through different plastic tunnels. Alisha is the smallest in our team and she is SO FAST, like a

speedy burrowing mole!

The final and **biggest** challenge is the timed circuit run. We all crowd around to study the map. Colored chalk signs mark the route.

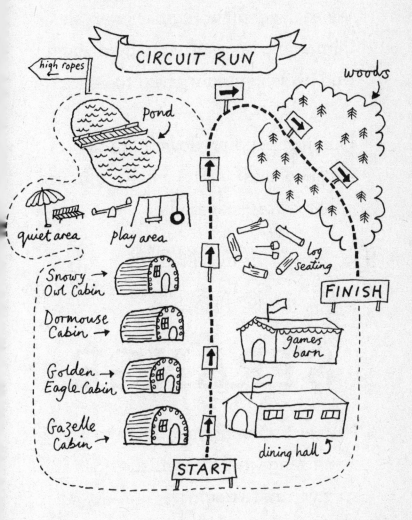

CIRCUIT RUN

high ropes

woods

Pond

high ropes

quiet area   play area

log seating

Snowy
Owl Cabin →

Dormouse
Cabin →

FINISH

Golden →
Eagle Cabin

games
barn

Gazelle
Cabin →

dining hall ↰

START

We each set off at regular intervals.
I am lining up, waiting to begin, and I
find myself standing next to Laura.

I am just bending down to re-tie
my shoelaces, when I catch a glimpse
of her *hands*—covered in

colored
chalk.

STRANGE.

I am just opening my mouth to say
something when the whistle goes and
it's my turn to begin.

I start out at a **_good pace,_**
and pass quite a few other runners.

I reach the sign

pointing

LEFT.

I run past the pond, away from the dark woods with the others close behind.

This isn't the **right** route, **surely???**

I think *puff puff*

There is something funny going on...

puff puff

Then it all clicked into place!

Someone has turned the signs around—just like in that episode of **FRED FANTASTIC!!!!!!!**

AND I KNOW WHO IT WAS...

BUT—it makes 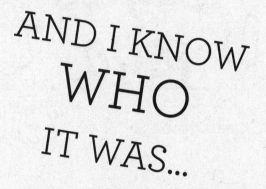 sense! How does this help Laura win the race?

I start running *faster* and *faster*— I must find Beans!

My heart is **pounding**
and my legs feel like

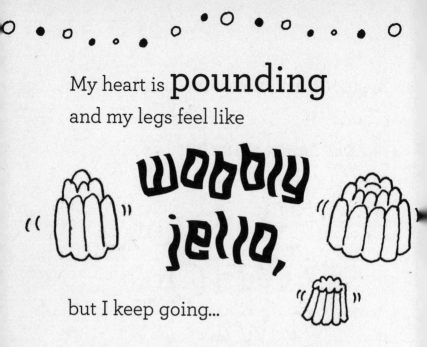

wobbly jello,

but I keep going...

And AT LAST I reach the finishing line.

The **Ace Adventure Helpers** use their stopwatches to work out our times. Everybody is rushing over to the scoreboard, but I am rushing in the **OPPOSITE DIRECTION** to find Beans.

It takes AGES, but at last I finally find him in the crowd.

I tell Beans about how Laura changed the signs to alter the running race route. It takes a while as I still have hardly got my breath back!

"But WHY???" he asks.

"Her team had to follow the same signs as we did—it didn't help them win. So why did she do it? **What IS she up to?**"

This case is a **HOT POTATO!** FRED FANTASTIC says this a lot. It doesn't mean it's a real potato...

It means it's a **super-tricky** problem.

And slowly it begins to dawn on me... Maybe we've got it wrong. Maybe it's not about the **ACE ADVENTURERS' PRIZE** at all.

"The answer is in the **clues** if only we

could just see it," I say. "Laura ruined my night-time campfire **spooky** story..."

"And she hid the flashlights to spoil the **moonlight** walk..." says Beans.

"And she made us run around the pond instead of through the **dark** woods," I say...

And suddenly I have a

LIGHT-BULB MOMENT!!!

"I've GOT it!

I KNOW what's happened!" I say. "Laura is afraid of

THE DARK!"

And we put together the pieces of the puzzle. So we were right all along about what Laura did, but not about WHY.

We rush over to Mr. D and tell him all about it.

Mr. D listens quietly, but he just says, "Just give me a few minutes." We see him walk with Laura over to the Quiet Area for a chat.

Now Mr. D and Laura are coming back over to us.

Laura looks at her shoes and says, very quietly, "I'm sorry I ruined the activities for everyone. I didn't want you all to know that I think the dark is **really scary**."

"But all those camps you've been to," I say, "night-kayaking in the Amazon, sleeping under the stars in the Arctic!"

Laura digs a little hole in the mud with her toe and says nothing. I now see that might have been a bit of an **exaggeration.**

I can't help feeling sorry for her.

So I say, "Well, not many people know this, but I used to be really **scared** of my robe, hanging on my bedroom door.

I thought it would

come to life

in the

night!"

I shudder. Beans pulls his t-shirt over his head and does a creepy *robe* dance around me. Laura smiles.

"Come on," says Beans, "they're announcing the **winners!**" and we all go over together.

Kirstie and Amy's team wins the **Ace Adventurers' Prize**, which they really deserve because they scored well on the activities, but also Amy was brave and Kirstie was kind.

We all **CLAP** and **CHEER.**

I see Laura clapping too.

I scored some extra points with my **super-fast running,** so our team is **second,** which is

PRETTY FANTASTIC!

Now it is time to pack our bags and get back on to the bus. With the Helpers waving us off, we head back home.

As we come around the corner and see our school, there are our families waiting for us.

McClusky is beside himself with **excitement** to see me!

Welcome home, Dot!

We are all very **GRUBBY** and **TIRED** and are walking a bit like

ZOMBIES.

Joe could not find his shorts anywhere and is wearing his pajama bottoms.

For a reason absolutely no one can explain, Frankie seems to be absent-mindedly wearing TWO pairs of shorts, one **on top** of the other.

Mr. D makes sure Joe is reunited with his shorts, Lily and Amber are wearing the right shoes, and Fiyaz has his tooth safely in his pocket...

And as the last of us are leaving...

I see Mr. D walking to his car to go home, and he does a little

dance of joy,

probably because he **loved** the school trip SO MUCH.

So tired, can hardly write a single word.

My own home. My own bed.

Saturday

Today is the

LARKS
IN THE
PARK Dog Show.

And here is McClusky's surprise— Mom has given him an AMAZING new **bow tie!** Made out of the pinwheel from his hoard of treasures!

(See, there IS a point keeping loads of stuff, I tell Mom.)

I brush McClusky's coat. He looks very cool with **slicked-back hair** and he is SO PROUD of his new bow tie.

Me and Beans go over to the dog show while Mom and the twins look at the homemade jams.

When we arrive, there are lots of dogs already waiting...

"Come on, McClusky, it's **starting!**"

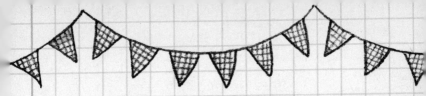

He parades beautifully in the

HANDSOMEST
HOUND

round, and wags his tail until it is an
absolute *blur*.

And now the trickiest round: the

Sausage-on-a-plate Race.

The contestants are lining up.

I give McClusky his plate and
his sausage. I stare at him **very
intensely** and he stares back.

"You can do it, McClusky!" I say.

Then the whistle is blown and they all start off.

But now lots of people crowd in front of me and I lose sight of McClusky.

I am hopping up and down, but I can't see over everybody's heads— it is **SO FRUSTATING**—until at last I hear the applause and cheers and the judge calls out:

"We HAVE A WINNER!"

Later, we are all sitting on the grass having ice creams. McClusky is wearing his BEST IN SHOW rosette.

"First place in the

Sausage-on-a-plate Race,

McClusky!" I say.

"He also scored points for being a **handsome hound** AND for his tail-wagging!" says Beans.

"His new bow tie must have given him lots of last-minute confidence," I say.

We talk about **THE CASE OF THE ACE ADVENTURERS' PRIZE.** This was our trickiest yet!

Another case...

JOIN
THE DOTS
DETECTIVES

What will our next fiendishly tricky
mystery be?

"It turns out that Laura isn't nearly as confident as she makes out," I say, "and Amy is getting **braver** every day!"

"Yes!" says Beans. And then he says, "I wonder what Norman is doing right now..."

Have you read?

When someone seems set on sabotaging the school show, Dot is determined to find out how, and save the day!

When Dot starts hearing strange noises at night, Beans is convinced there has to be something SPOOKY afoot. But before they can be certain, Dot and Beans must GET PROOF.

Join Dot, Beans, and McClusky
on their next case...

coming soon...

The end